Surprise! Surprise!

NIKI DALY

Otter-Barry BOOKS

Mr and Mrs Tati lived in a little yellow house
with a red tin roof.

Inside the house they had
almost all they needed to be happy –

a stove,   good food,   a table and
two chairs,

and a little red hen that laid eggs.

To Leo - thanks for the surprise!

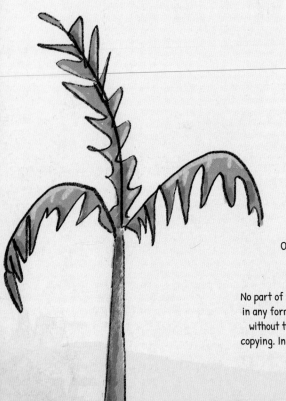

First published in Great Britain in 2017 by
Otter-Barry Books, Little Orchard, Burley Gate, Herefordshire, HR1 3QS

A catalogue record for this book is available from the British Library.

ISBN 978-1-91095-999-2

Illustrated with digital art

Printed in China

They also had a **big** comfy bed

and a tiny blue radio that played happy music.

There was only one thing missing...

Mr Tati couldn't **bear** his wife to be unhappy.
So he went to a Baby Shop to buy a baby.

"I'm looking for a fat, happy baby for
dear Mrs Tati," he explained to the lady
in the Baby Shop.

"I'm afraid we have no babies," replied the lady,
"only baby cots, baby prams, baby bottles,
baby nappies and baby bottom powder."

"Oh dear," sighed Mr Tati, "those things will be
of no use without a baby." And he left the shop.

On his way home he passed a man selling baby pigs.
If we *can't* have a baby, thought Mr Tati, perhaps a
little **pink pig** will make dear Mrs Tati happy.

So Mr Tati bought a pink pig with
fat baby cheeks and took him home.

When Mrs Tati saw what a lovely little pink pig Mr Tati had brought home, she clapped her hands.

"What a beautiful piggy!" she cried.

"I do **love** him!"

And because he was as **round** as a pot
they called him Potter.

Immediately, Mrs Tati knitted
a **blue** and **pink** baby jumper,

yellow baby booties

and a **red** baby beanie.

And because Potter was so little,
Mr Tati said he should sleep
with them in the big comfy bed.

And because he was much too tiny
to be left alone, Mrs Tati carried him
everywhere she went.

After a while, Mr and Mrs Tati began to think of Potter as their little boy. Mrs Tati was very happy. Mr Tati was happy, too.

And Potter was as happy as a piggy wrapped in a soft baby blanket can be.

And so life went on until the day arrived
when Potter was old enough to start school.
Mr Tati worked extra hard to buy him –

a smart shirt and shorts,

shiny black school shoes,

a little brown suitcase,

a lunch box,

crayons and two school books -
one for drawing in and one for reading.

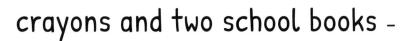

But when they took him to school, Miss Prim, the headmistress, said, "This is a school for little boys and girls. I'm afraid **little pigs** are NOT allowed."

Mr and Mrs Tati were terribly upset.
It had been a **BIG** mistake trying to
turn a little pig into a little boy.

So instead of going to school,
Potter was allowed
to play in a muddy puddle

and sleep under the stars on a bed of straw.

But for a special weekend treat, he was given a warm bubble bath, put into fancy pyjamas, and allowed to climb into the big comfy bed between Mr and Mrs Tati.

And there they listened to happy music played on the tiny blue radio until it was time to turn off the light.

But in the dark, when Potter was fast asleep, Mrs Tati would whisper to Mr Tati, "Oh, I wish, I wish our little pig had **ten sweet toes** like yours."

"And **ten sweet fingers** to match!" Mr Tati would add.

"And a **button-size nose** like mine would be lovely too," said Mrs Tati.

"With tiny ears like mine to match," said Mr Tati.

"And what about a little round bottom **without** a piggy-wiggy tail?" Mrs Tati whispered.

"He'd be just like us, and we'd all be the same," Mr Tati whispered back very softly.

"Oh, I wish, I wish, I wish, I wish..."
Mrs Tati wished sadly before she fell asleep.

Mr Tati couldn't **bear** his wife to be unhappy.
So one starlit night he went outside
and wished upon a falling star.

"I wish, I wish, I wish,
that when we wake up in the morning...
we will **all** look the same."

Surprise!

A
very
happy
ending.